A Note to Parents and Caregivers:

With a focus on math, science, and social studies, *Read-it!* Readers support both the learning of content information and the extension of more complex reading skills. They encourage the development of problem-solving skills that help children expand their thinking.

 The PURPLE LEVEL presents basic topics and objects using high frequency words and simple language patterns.

 The RED LEVEL presents familiar topics using common words and repeating sentence patterns.

 The BLUE LEVEL presents new ideas using a larger vocabulary and varied sentence structure.

 The YELLOW LEVEL presents more challenging ideas, a broad vocabulary, and wide variety in sentence structure.

 The GREEN LEVEL presents more complex ideas, an extended vocabulary range, and expanded language structures.

 The ORANGE LEVEL presents a wide range of ideas and concepts using challenging vocabulary and complex language structures.

When sharing a content focused book with your child, read to find out facts and concepts, pausing often to restate and talk about the new information. The realistic story format provides an opportunity to talk about the language used, and to learn about reading to problem-solve for information. Encourage children to measure, make maps, and consider other situations that allow them to apply what they are learning.

There is no right or wrong way to share books with children. Find time to read and share new learning with your child, and pass on the legacy of literacy.

Adria F. Klein, Ph.D.
Professor Emeritus
California State University
San Bernardino, California

D0109088

Editor: Christianne Jones
Designers: Hilary Wacholz and Amy Muehlenhardt
Page Production: Michelle Biedscheid
Art Director: Nathan Gassman
The illustrations in this book were created digitally.

Picture Window Books
5115 Excelsior Boulevard
Suite 232
Minneapolis, MN 55416
877-845-8392
www.picturewindowbooks.com

Printed in the United States of America.

Library of Congress Cataloging-in-Publication Data
Aboff, Marcie.
Mike's mystery / by Marcie Aboff ; illustrated by Amy Bailey Muehlenhardt.
p. cm. — (Read-it! readers. Math)
ISBN-13: 978-1-4048-3667-9 (library binding)
ISBN-13: 978-1-4048-3671-6 (paperback)
1. Subtraction—Juvenile literature. 2. Friendship—Juvenile literature. 3. Books—
Juvenile literature. I. Muehlenhardt, Amy Bailey, 1974-, ill. II. Title.
QA115.A264 2008
513.2'12—dc22   2007004069

Mike's Mystery

Hi Tanner -

It's no
mystery,
you're great!

by Marcie Aboff
illustrated by Amy Bailey Muehlenhardt

Special thanks to our advisers for their expertise:

Stuart Farm, M.Ed.
Mathematics Lecturer, University of North Dakota
Grand Forks, North Dakota

Adria F. Klein, Ph.D.
Professor Emeritus, California State University
San Bernardino, California

PICTURE WINDOW BOOKS
Minneapolis, Minnesota

Mike loved to read. He read all kinds
of books. He read about kings and queens.

He read about cats with big hats.

He read about stars and spaceships.

Mike's favorite books were called *Dino Spy, Private Eye*. They were about a dinosaur who solved mysteries.

One day at school, Mrs. Harris told the class about the school's book drive.

"We will be collecting books to give to other children," she said. "Our classroom goal is to donate seventy-five books. That's five books per student. If we reach our goal, we'll have a pizza party."

"Let's work together and try to donate twenty-nine books," said Ned.

"Why twenty-nine?" Mike asked.

"It's my favorite number," Ned said.

"I'm in," said Sara. "We'll get a pizza party for sure if the three of us donate so many books."

After school, Sara and Ned brought boxes of books over to Mike's house.

"I know we can find twenty-nine books to donate out of all of these," said Sara.

Dino Spy, Private Eye

Book 3

"Some younger kids might like these shorter books," Mike said.

He put five books in a pile. Mike, Ned, and Sara subtracted five books from twenty-nine. They still needed twenty-four to reach their goal.

29 - 5 = 24

Sara picked up one of Mike's *Dino Spy* books.

"I love this series!" said Sara. "I have all four *Dino Spy* books."

"So do I," said Mike. "But these books are special. The author signed them for me."

"Wow, you're so lucky!" said Sara. "I wish my books were signed."

Mike, Sara, and Ned spent the next hour sorting through all of their books.

"I know someone will like these three animal books," Sara told Mike and Ned. "Twenty-four minus three equals twenty-one."

"These eleven science books should help us reach our goal," said Ned.

21 - 11 = 10

"That leaves us with a difference of ten books," said Mike.

"I don't think we have ten more books to donate," said Sarah.

Just then, Mike's sister Beth walked into the room. She had a pile of chapter books.

"I already have ten books to donate to my class," said Beth. "I thought you might want to look through my extra books."

"Thank you, Beth," Sarah said. "If we take ten of your books, we'll reach our goal."

10 - 10 = 0

"I know our class will hit the goal now," said Ned.

"I hope so," said Mike. "I can taste the pizza already!"

After everyone left, Beth took her extra books back to her room. Mike started to put his extra books away, too. But something was missing. *Dino Spy, Private Eye—Book 3* was not there! Mike searched through all of the books in his bookcase.

He looked behind the bookcase.

He checked under his bed.

He looked under his dresser.

He even called his friends. His book was gone! Where could it be?

At school the next day, all of the kids brought in their books to donate.

Mike told Mrs. Harris about his missing book. She said he could look through the donated books.

At recess, while the other kids were playing outside, Mike stayed inside to look for his book. "I'll help you look," Sara told Mike.

There were tables and tables full of books in the gym. It took Mike and Sara a long time to search through all of the books.

"Here's a *Dino Spy* book!" Sara yelled.

Mike opened it up. "There's no autograph," he said.

There was another *Dino Spy* book, but that wasn't Mike's, either. They never found Mike's book.

"Too bad we couldn't find your book,"
said Sara. "I'd be sad if I lost my book, too."
"Thanks for helping me look," Mike told Sara.

When Mike got home, he searched through
all of his books again. Mike kept thinking about
the last time he saw the book. Sara was in his
room. Ned was in his room. His sister was in his
room, too.

"Wait a minute!" Mike suddenly shouted. He ran to his sister's room. Beth's books were piled high on her desk. Mike picked up her books one by one. When he reached the bottom of the pile, Mike found his missing book.

Dino Spy, Private Eye

Book 3

"I didn't even know I had it!" Beth said.

"You must have picked it up when you took your books away with you," Mike said.

Mike felt like a private eye—just like Dino! Later that night, Mike had another idea.

The next day, Mike brought the book to school. He told Sara what happened.

"Let's exchange our *Dino Spy* books," Mike told Sara.

"But your book is signed," Sara said.

"I know," Mike said. "But I want you to have it. You spent a lot of time helping me look for it."

"Wow! Thanks!" Sara said.

Just then, Mrs. Harris came in and announced the final book count. "Instead of donating seventy-five books, our class donated ninety-five. That's twenty more than our goal! Bring in the pizza!"

95

- 75

20

95

"Being a private eye was so much work that I completely forgot about the pizza," said Mike.

"It's time to stop being a private eye and start being a kid again," said Ned.

"I agree," said Mike as he took a big bite of pizza.

Subtraction Activity

Mike loves to read. There are three shelves of books on his bookcase. Count the number of books on each shelf. Then subtract the number given in the math problem. How many books are left on each shelf after you subtract?

$? - 3 = ?$

$? - 7 = ?$

$? - 12 = ?$

Answer key: 14-3 = 11, 9-7 = 2, 19-12 = 7

Glossary

difference—the amount left after one amount is subtracted from another

equals—being the same in amount

minus—take away

subtract—to take away from

To Learn More

At the Library

Cleary, Brian P. *The Action of Subtraction*. Minneapolis: Millbrook Press, 2006.
Kassirer, Sue. *Math Fair Blues*. New York: Kane Press, 2001.
Leedy, Loreen. *Subtraction Action*. New York: Holiday House, 2000.
Penner, Lucille Recht. *Lights Out!* New York: Kane Press, 2000.

On the Web

FactHound offers a safe, fun way to find Web sites related to this book. All of the sites on FactHound have been researched by our staff.

1. Visit *www.facthound.com*
2. Type in this special code: 1404836675
3. Click on the FETCH IT button.

Your trusty FactHound will fetch the best sites for you!

Look for all of the books in the *Read-it!* Readers: Math series:

The Lemonade Standoff (math: two-digit addition without regrouping)
Mike's Mystery (math: two-digit subtraction without regrouping)
The Pizza Palace (math: fractions)
The Tallest Snowman (math: measurements)